Mrs.

S0-AGB-993

Ernie's Telephone Call

Ernie's Telephone Call

BY RAY SIPHERD
PICTURES BY IRRA DUGA

Featuring Jim Henson's Muppets

A SESAME STREET BOOK

Published by Western Publishing Company, Inc., in cooperation with Children's
Television Workshop. © 1978 Children's Television Workshop. Muppet characters
© 1971, 1978 Muppets, Inc. All rights reserved. Produced in U.S.A. Ernie is a
trademark of Muppets, Inc. Sesame Street® and the Sesame Street sign are
trademarks and service marks of Children's Television Workshop. WHITMAN and
TELL-A-TALE are registered trademarks of Western Publishing Company, Inc. No part
of this book may be reproduced or copied in any form without written permission from
the publisher.

"I'll answer the telephone, Bert," called Ernie.

"Hello?" he said, after picking up the receiver. "No, I didn't hear what happened to you today. Tell me. What was it?"

"This morning you were happy because you went on a picnic? . . . And the weather was great? . . . And you had baloney sandwiches and soda and cake?"

"And you played softball and hit a home run? No wonder you were HAPPY! It makes *me* happy just to hear about it!"

"So you grabbed your baloney sandwich and ran under a tree. . . . And then you were really sad because the picnic was ruined. Gee! It makes me sad, too."

"And while you were standing there, you were SURPRISED to see climbing down toward you . . . A GIANT GORILLA!"

"And the gorilla reached down and grabbed your baloney sandwich! ... And then you got angry!"

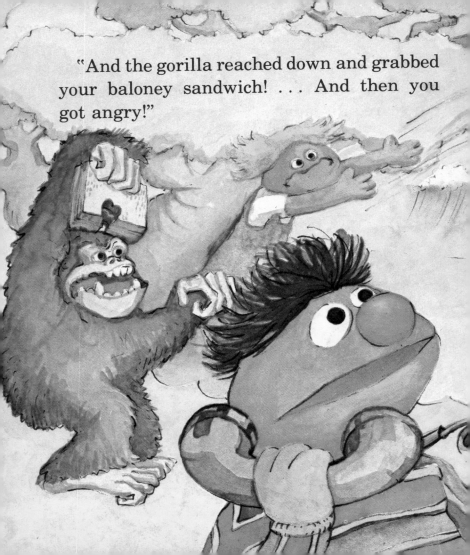

"Then the gorilla said he was sorry? And to show you he was friendly, he picked you up and carried you on his shoulders? ... And when everybody saw how you had made friends with a giant gorilla, they cheered? ... And you felt very PROUD? Boy, I'd feel proud, too!"

"What's that? . . . Really? . . . Oh, that's all right. It was nice talking to you, anyway. Good-bye."

"Wait a minute, Ernie," said Bert. "Let me get this straight. You were just talking to somebody who was HAPPY at a picnic . . .

" . . . then who was SAD because it started to rain and the picnic was ruined . . .

"...then who was SURPRISED when a giant gorilla appeared...

"...then who was AFRAID because the gorilla had big eyes and sharp teeth...

". . . then who was ANGRY because the gorilla grabbed the baloney sandwich . . .

". . . and who was PROUD when they made friends and everybody cheered!

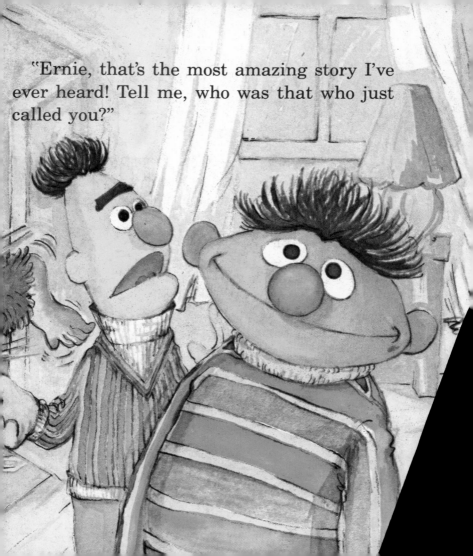

"Ernie, that's the most amazing story I've ever heard! Tell me, who was that who just called you?"

"Gee, Bert, I don't know. It was a wrong number."